Super-Duper Science

Rain, Rain,
Go Away!

by Annalisa McMorrow
illustrated by Marilynn G. Barr

For Sarah & Scobie

Publisher: Roberta Suid
Design & Production: Scott McMorrow
Educational Consultant: Sarah Felstiner
Cover Art: Mike Artell

Also by the author:
Holiday Crafts (MM 935), *Save the Animals!* (MM 1964), *Love the Earth!*
(MM 1965), *Learn to Recycle!* (MM 1966), *Sing a Song about Animals* (MM
1987), *Preschool Connections* (MM 1993), *Ladybug Ladybug* (MM 2015),
Twinkle, Twinkle (MM 2016), *Rub-a-Dub-Dub* (MM 2017), *Incredible Insects!*
(MM 2018), *Spectacular Space!* (MM 2019), and *Outstanding Oceans!*
(MM 2020).

For a complete catalog, please write to the address below:
P.O. Box 1680, Palo Alto, CA 94302
or call: 1-800-255-6048

Please visit our web site: http//www.mondaymorningbooks.com

or e-mail us at MMBooks@aol.com

ISBN 1-57612-010-4

Printed in the United States of America
987654321

Contents

Introduction   4

All About Weather   6

Chapter 1: Clouds   7

Chapter 2: Rain (& Rainbows)   19

Chapter 3: Wind   33

Chapter 4: Snow   47

Chapter 5: Sunny Days   61

Weather Watcher's Guide   74

Storybook Resources   78

Nonfiction Resources   80

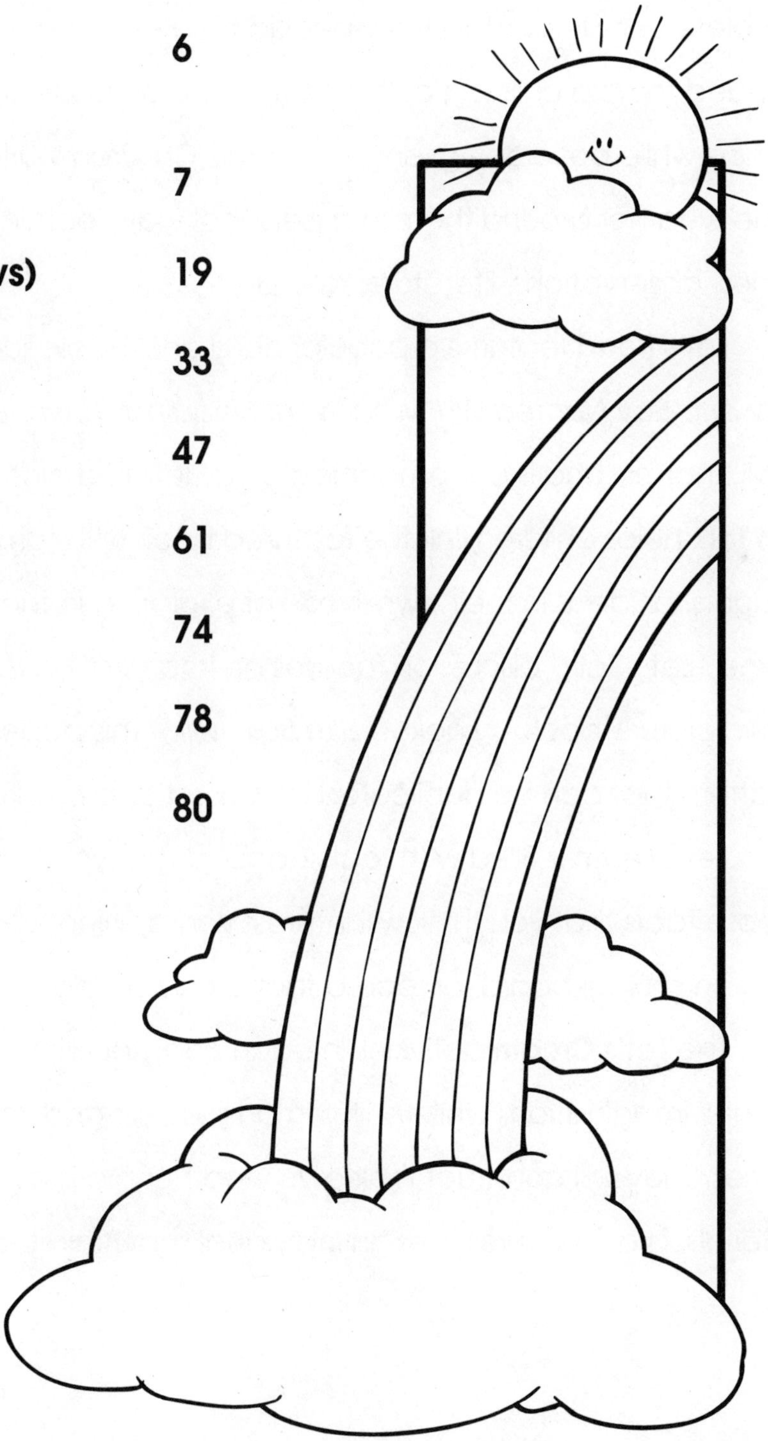

Introduction

Rain, Rain, Go Away! is composed of five chapters, each a complete unit dedicated to a specific type of weather. This book is intended to help children cultivate a hands-on understanding of science while developing language skills. Children will learn to relate to the weather around them in a personal way: learning through games, observations, literature, and art.

Let's Read features a popular children's book, such as *The Story of a Boy Named Will, Who Went Sledding Down the Hill* by Daniil Kharms, and is accompanied by a detailed plot description. **Let's Talk** helps children link the featured book with familiar feelings, thoughts, or ideas in their own lives. For example, in the Cloud chapter, the "Let's Talk" discussion focuses on imagination (featured in the classic picture book, *It Looked Like Spilt Milk*). This page also includes a pattern that can be duplicated and used as a bookmark.

Let's Learn is filled with facts about each type of weather. Choose facts that you think will interest your students. You can write these on a chalkboard, or read a fact a day during the unit.

The **Let's Create** activities in each chapter allow children to use their imaginations while building artistic skills and fine-motor abilities. They will construct their own weather pictures from craft materials, draw pictures, design individual snowflakes, and so on.

Children make a hands-on science connection in the **Let's Find Out** activities. These projects focus on exploration, leading children through moments of discovery as they *find out* how to make a shadow or create a rainbow.

Let's Play suggests a new game (or games) to interest children in the weather of the moment. (Note: Directions often suggest covering game pieces with Contac paper for extra durability. You can use any type of clear, adhesive paper to cover the game pieces. Laminator machines can also be used.)

A chant or a new song sung to a familiar tune is featured in the **Let's Sing** section. Children can learn the lyrics and put on performances for parents, teachers, or each other. Mother Goose rhymes are also included.

Informative **Pattern Pages** complete each chapter. These patterns can be duplicated and used for bulletin board displays, reduced for cubby labels or name tags, or used for desk labeling. Children can color the patterns using crayons or markers. Provide glue and glitter for a bit of extra sparkle.

At the end of the book, you'll find a **Weather Watcher's Guide**, which includes weather icons (p. 74), weather gear icons (p. 75), and calendar patterns (pp. 76-77). You'll also find a **Storybook Resources** section filled with additional fiction picture books, plus a **Nonfiction Resources** section suggesting factual books of the featured types of weather.

ALL ABOUT WEATHER

What Is Weather?

When you breathe in, you take air into your lungs. When you blow up a balloon, you fill it with air. Air is made up of several gasses. A gas is something you usually can't see but that you can feel and sometimes smell. Weather is the study of the air around us. It deals with wind, rain, temperature, and dirt. People who study weather are called meteorologists.

Wind is moving air. When we want to know about the weather, we ask many questions about air movement: Is the air calm or is it blowing? If it's blowing, how fast is it going? A strong wind makes kites fly and sailboats move. A very strong wind can be dangerous.

Temperature is a measure of heat. The air can be cold, cool, warm, or hot. No one temperature is better than another. Cold air is needed if you want to go sledding. Hot air makes vegetables grow. The wind doesn't change the temperature, but it does change how it feels to people. If it's very cold outside, a fast wind can make your skin feel even colder!

CLOUDS

Introduction

• Let's Read:
It Looked Like Spilt Milk by Charles G. Shaw (HarperCollins, 1947). Each page of this bright blue and white book shows a cloud in an identifiable shape. Children will enjoy looking at the pictures and calling out the shapes. This classic picture book is now available as a board book, too.

• Let's Talk:
After reading *It Looked Like Spilt Milk,* plan a cloud-watching day. On a day when there are clouds in the sky, take the children outside. Have them look at the clouds. Do they see any images?

• Let's Learn:
Look for these three types of clouds with the children: cumulus, stratus, and cirrus. Cumulus clouds are large puffs of warm air that float upward. They are often dark. Sometimes cumulus clouds in the sky mean there is going to be a storm. Stratus clouds look like large flat blankets covering the sky. Cirrus clouds can look like feathers or frost on a window. They are so high in the sky that the water in them freezes into ice crystals. Cirrus clouds are often called ice clouds. See the patterns (p. 18) for drawings of these cloud types.

Refer to the **Nonfiction Resources** for additional books about clouds.

7

CLOUDS

Let's Create: Silver Linings

An old proverb states: Every cloud has a silver lining. Your children can make that proverb come true.

What You Need:

"We're Clouds" pattern (p. 18), silver glitter, glue, small cups, cotton swabs, scissors, construction paper (in a variety of blue shades)

What You Do:

1. Duplicate a copy of the cloud patterns for each child. Duplicate and enlarge one copy to use for this lesson.
2. Discuss the different types of clouds while pointing to them on the enlarged pattern.
3. Have the children cut out the cloud patterns and glue them to sheets of construction paper.
4. Provide a mixture of silver glitter and glue in small cups.
5. Demonstrate how to use the cotton swabs to paint with the glitter/glue mixture. Children can use this to outline the clouds.
6. Post the completed pictures on an "Every Cloud Has a Silver Lining" bulletin board.

Option:

• Ask the children what they think "Every cloud has a silver lining" means. (It's okay if children have different ideas.) One definition to share: Good things can come out of unpleasant experiences, for example, a rainbow after a rainy day.

CLOUDS

Let's Create: Sponge Clouds

What You Need:
Sponges, white and gray tempera paint (in pie tins), blue construction paper, scissors, newsprint

What You Do:
1. Cover the work area with newsprint.
2. Cut the sponges into cloud shapes. (If you need help, refer to the patterns on page 18.)
3. Provide white and gray tempera paint in tins for children to share.
4. Demonstrate how to sponge print cloud shapes onto the blue paper. Children can drag the sponges on their papers, or lift up the sponges each time they make imprints. Suggest that children group their prints together in "cloud" shapes, leaving some blue.
5. Post the completed pictures at children's eye level around the classroom.

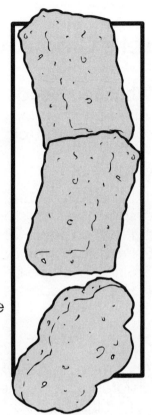

Options:
• Have children work together to sponge print a mural using a large sheet of butcher paper for the background. Children can use brushes to paint the butcher paper using blue paint first.
• Provide crayons or markers for children to use to decorate the clouds once they've dried.

Book Link:
• *The Cloud Book* by Tomie de Paola (Holiday House, 1975). Teach children the ten most common types of clouds with facts (and myths) from this book.

CLOUDS

Let's Create: Cotton Ball Clouds

What You Need:
White construction paper, cotton balls, glue or glue sticks, scissors, clothesline, clothespins

What You Do:
1. Let children cut cloud shapes from white construction paper. (If they need assistance, duplicate copies of the "We're Clouds" pattern on page 18 for use as templates.)
2. Provide cotton balls for children to glue to their cloud shapes.
3. String a length of clothesline across the classroom.
4. Hang the completed clouds from the clothesline using clothespins.

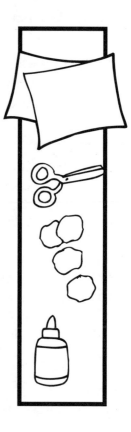

Option:
After reading *It Looked Like Spilt Milk* or *Hello, Clouds!*, have children observe the cotton ball clouds and share what shapes they think the clouds look like.

Book Link:
• *Hello, Clouds* by Dalia Hardof Renberg, illustrated by Alona Frankel (Harper & Row, 1985).
A child describes the many different items a cloud can look like.

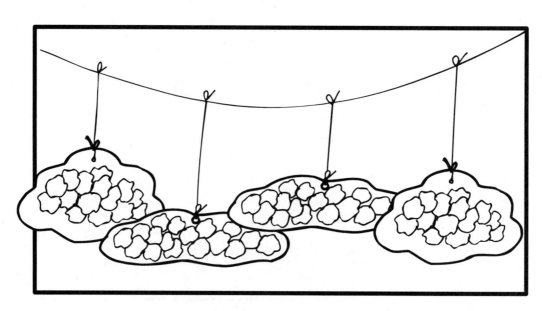

CLOUDS

Let's Create: Pudding Clouds

Have children wash their hands before doing this activity!

What You Need:

"We're Clouds" pattern (p. 18), vanilla pudding, colored paper plates (one per child), smocks, plastic spoons

What You Do:

1. Duplicate and enlarge a copy of the "We're Clouds" pattern.
2. Make vanilla pudding according to directions on the box.
3. Place a small amount of pudding on each plate.
4. Let the children fingerpaint using the pudding. They can make clouds that look like the ones on the pattern, or they can make their own shapes.

Options:

• Provide vanilla pudding for children to eat during snack time after finishing this activity.
• Provide marshmallow fluff for children to use to sculpt clouds.

CLOUDS

Let's Find Out: About Different Types of Clouds

Do this activity after reading *It Looked Like Spilt Milk.*

What You Need:

"We're Clouds" pattern (p. 18)

What You Do:

1. Duplicate a copy of the "We're Clouds" pattern for each child.
2. On a day when there are clouds in the sky, take the children outside with their patterns.
3. Have the children look at the clouds and see if they can identify any of the cloud types. They can use the patterns to identify different types of clouds.

Option:

• Make a chart of the different types of clouds children see or the number of clouds children see.

Book Link:

• *The Weather Sky* by Bruce McMillan (Farrar, 1991).
This nonfiction resource features color photographs of many different types of clouds. It also includes explanations about what type of weather conditions are necessary for different cloud types.

CLOUDS

Let's Play: Cloud Jumping

What You Need:
Game Pieces & Spinner (p. 14), Game Board pattern (p. 15), crayons or markers, Contac paper, scissors, hole punch, brad

What You Do:
1. Duplicate the Game Board pattern, Game Pieces, and Spinner.
2. Color all game parts and cover with Contac paper.
3. Punch a hole in the center of the spinner. Cut out and attach the arrow using a brad.
4. Explain the game to the students. Three players may play at a time. The object of the game is for the children to jump from cloud to cloud until they reach the final cloud. The first child spins the spinner and moves to the next similarly shaped spot on the board. The first child to land at the spot marked "end" is the winner.

Option:
• Cut out large cloud shapes from white paper and place on the floor. Challenge children to hop from one cloud to another.

GAME PIECES & SPINNER

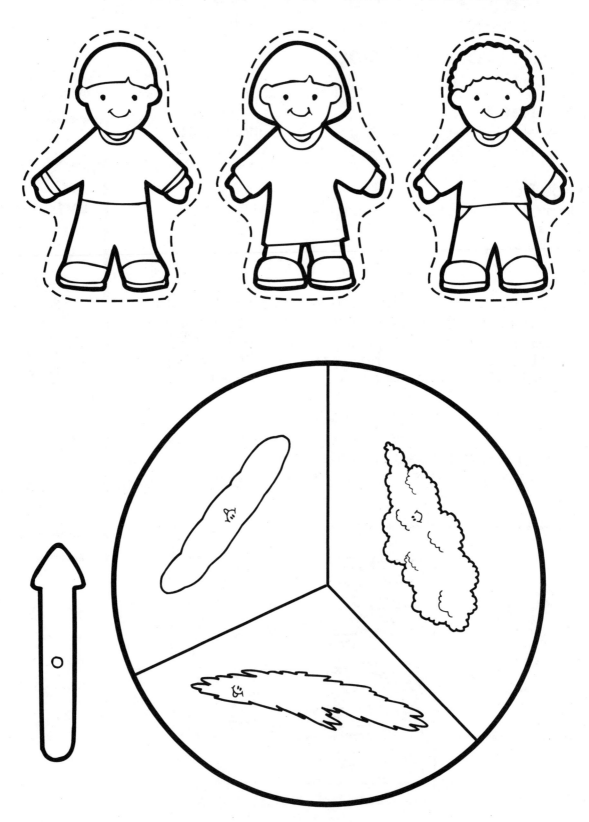

GAME BOARD PATTERN

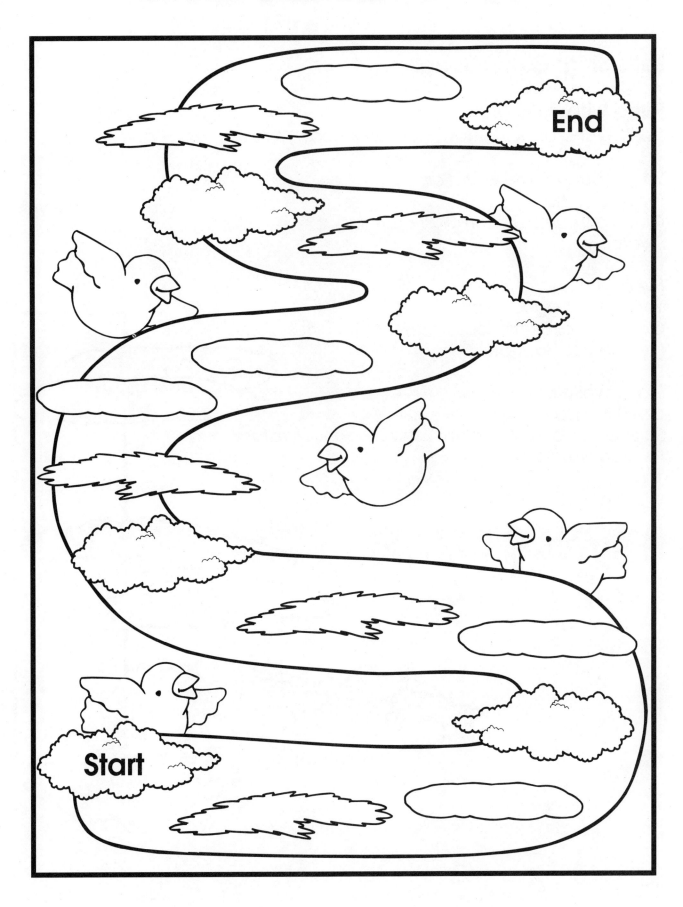

CLOUDS

Let's Sing: Cloud Songs

Filled with Puffs of Air
(to the tune of "Row, Row, Row Your Boat")

You're puffed with warm air,
Way up in the sky.
Cumulus, cumulus, cumulus, cumulus,
I watch you float by.

Filled with crystal ice.
You have ragged sides.
Cirrus cloud, cirrus cloud, cirrus cloud, cirrus cloud,
I watch you float by.

Like a white blanket
Covering up the sky.
Stratus cloud, stratus cloud, stratus cloud, stratus cloud,
I watch you float by.

CLOUDS

Let's Learn: Mother Goose Rhymes

One Misty, Moisty Morning

One misty, moisty, morning,
When cloudy was the weather,
I chanced to meet an old man
Clothed all in leather,
With a strap beneath his chin.
How do you do, and how do you do,
And how do you do again?

When the Clouds Are Upon the Hills

When the clouds are upon the hills,
They'll come down by the mills.

When Clouds Appear

When clouds appear like rocks and towers,
The earth's refresh'd by frequent showers.

WE'RE CLOUDS

stratus

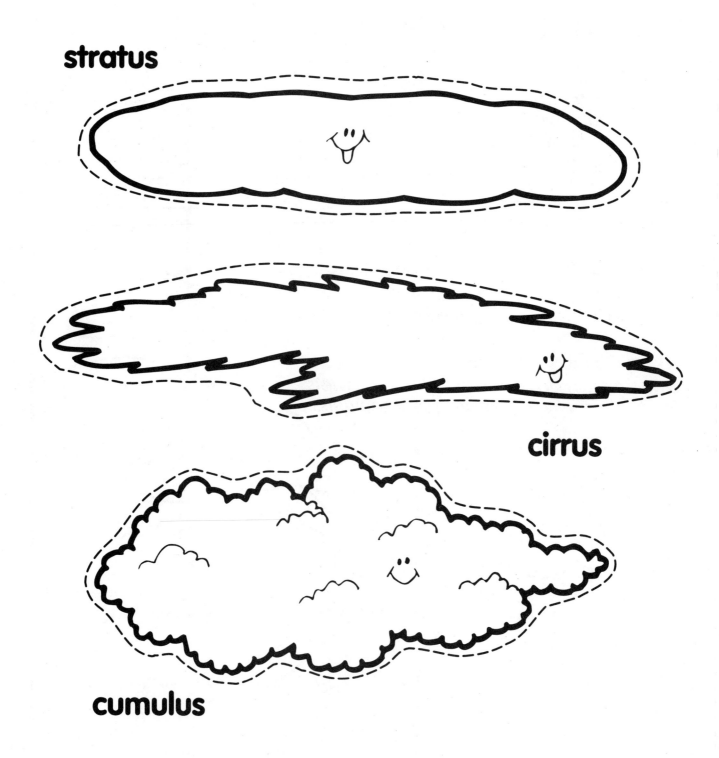

cirrus

cumulus

RAIN

Introduction

• Let's Read:
Rain by Peter Spier (Doubleday, 1982).
In this wordless book, two children explore their neighborhood during a rain shower. They splash through puddles and make mud footprints until the strong wind drives them home.

• Let's Talk:
After sharing this book with the children, have them help you put words to the story. Page through the book a second time, having the children discuss what is going on in each page. Then ask children to tell about their own experiences on rainy days. Do they like rain? Do they think it would be fun to do what the children in the story did?

• Let's Learn:
Rain clouds are darker than other clouds because they are filled with water droplets. No sunlight can shine through them. Different-sized raindrops fall from different clouds. Small raindrops fall from stratus clouds. Larger raindrops fall from cumulonimbus clouds. As raindrops fall, they don't look like our idea of raindrops. They actually look like tiny hamburger buns! When they land and drip down our window panes, they take on the teardrop shape we are familiar with.

RAIN

Let's Create: An Animal Storm

Teach children the description, "It's raining cats and dogs." Have children share their thoughts about what this might mean. (Write down all of the children's ideas.) Explain that this is one way of saying it is raining very heavily.

What You Need:

Cats and Dogs patterns (p. 21), colored construction paper, colored chalk, crayons, scissors, hole punches (paper circles left over from hole punching), glue

What You Do:

1. Duplicate a copy of the Cats and Dogs patterns for each child to color and cut out.
2. Provide craft materials for children to use to create stormy pictures. White and black chalk can be swirled together to make angry looking clouds. Hole punches can be glued on for rain.
3. Have children glue the animal patterns to their rain pictures.
4. Post the completed pictures on an "It's Raining Cats and Dogs" bulletin board.

CATS AND DOGS PATTERNS

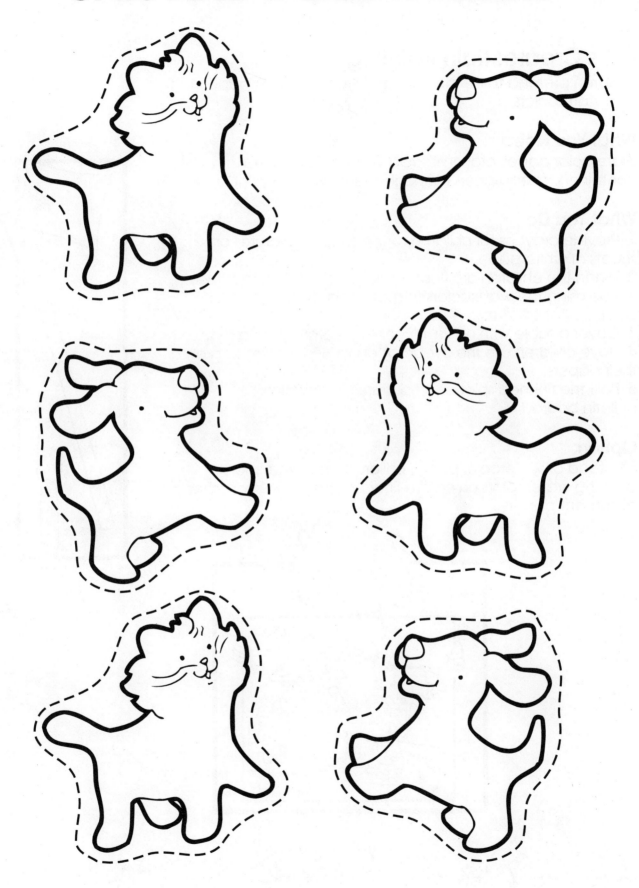

RAIN

Let's Create: Rain Painting

Children pretend to be the rain, and "rain" on their papers with watercolors.

What You Need:

Watercolor paper, crayons, liquid watercolors in small containers, eyedroppers (enough to share), newsprint

What You Do:

1. Provide crayons for children to use to draw pictures on sheets of white paper.
2. When the children are finished drawing, explain that they will be using the watercolors to make rain designs on their paper.
3. Cover a table with newsprint for the watercolor station.
4. Have children use the eyedroppers to drip watercolors onto their papers.
5. Post the finished splatter art pictures on a wall or bulletin board.

Option:

• Instead of watercolor paper, children can experiment dripping watercolors on coffee filters, paper towels, or other absorbent papers.

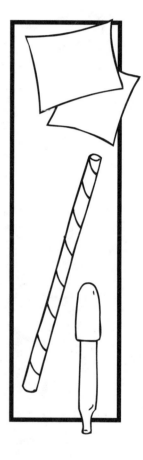

RAIN

Let's Create: Magical Moonbows

Sometimes raindrops catch the reflection of moonlight to form a moonbow. Moonbows are fainter than rainbows, but their colors appear in the same order and they are the same shape.

What You Need:

Black construction paper, oil pastels or chalk (in rainbow colors)

What You Do:

1. Explain the concept of a moonbow to the children.
2. Provide colored chalk for children to make moonbow pictures. Help them organize the colors in correct rainbow order (red, orange, yellow, green, blue, purple).
3. Post the completed pictures on a "Magical Moonbows" bulletin board.

Option:

• Spray the completed pictures with hair spray (a great chalk fixative). Make sure to do this away from the children!

Note:

Teach children the mnemonic for remembering the order of colors in the rainbow: **Roy G. Biv** (red, orange, yellow, green, blue, indigo, violet). The colors of the rainbow are always in this order.

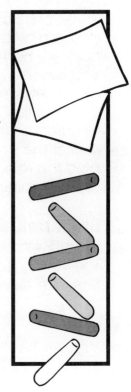

RAIN

Let's Create: Rain Thoughts

What You Need:
"We're Raindrops!" pattern (p. 32), pen

What You Do:
1. Duplicate the "We're Raindrops!" pattern, making one raindrop per child.
2. Ask children to share their feelings about rain with you. Prompt children by asking questions, such as "Do you like rain?" "Are you happy when it rains?" "Do you like playing in rain puddles?" "Do you have favorite rain gear to wear when it rains?" "What gets wet when it rains?"
3. Transcribe each child's feelings about rain on an individual raindrop pattern.
4. Post the patterns on a "Rainy Day Thoughts" bulletin board, or bind the raindrops in a class book. (Punch a hole through the top of each raindrop and fasten together using one long brad.)

Book Link:
• *Umbrella* by Taro Yashima (Viking, 1958).
The young girl in this story receives an umbrella for her birthday. She can't wait to use it, but she must wait for it to rain!

RAIN

Let's Create: A Rainbow Circle

Rainbows are curved because they are part of a circle. If you rode in an airplane over a rainstorm, you could see a complete, circular rainbow.

What You Need:
Butcher paper, tempera paint in rainbow colors (in pie tins), paintbrushes, newsprint

What You Do:
1. Cover the work area with newsprint.
2. Spread a large sheet of butcher paper over the newsprint and fasten the ends with masking tape.
3. Explain that the children will be making a full rainbow mural. (Discuss the fact that a rainbow is part of a circle.)
4. Help children start the mural by painting a large red circle on the butcher paper.
5. Have children work together to add the rest of the circles of colors, working inward after the red: orange, yellow, green, blue, indigo, and violet.
6. Once the rainbow circle is dry, write the children's name inside the circle and post the completed picture.

Options:
• Duplicate the "I'm a Rainbow!" pattern (p. 31) and color it using the appropriate order of colors. Post this in the room.
• Teach children the following Mother Goose riddle!

Purple, Yellow, Red, and Green
Purple, yellow, red, and green,
The king cannot reach it, nor yet the queen'
Nor can Old Noll, whose power's so great;
Tell me this riddle while I count eight.
(Answer: a rainbow)

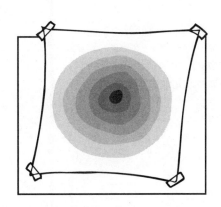

RAIN

Let's Find Out: About Rainbows

Do this activity on a bright, sunny day!

What You Need:
A garden hose

What You Do:
1. Explain that two things are needed for a rainbow to appear: sunlight and water droplets. Light reflects in the water droplets to make the colors of the rainbow.
2. Have the children stand with their backs to the sun.
3. Spray the garden hose in a fine mist in front of the children.
4. Children should look at the spray from the hose in a 45 degree angle. (You may need to have another adult assist children in finding the rainbow in the spray of the hose.)

Note:
When you look for rainbows, look at the opposite side of the sky to the sun. That's where rainbows always appear.

Options:
• Hang a prism in the window of the classroom. Have children be on the lookout for the time of day when rainbows fill the room!
• Shine a flashlight through a prism to make a rainbow.

Book Link:
• *A Rainbow of My Own* by Don Freeman (Viking, 1966). A little boy sees a rainbow and decides to try and catch it.

RAIN

Let's Find Out: Thunder and Lightning

This activity is only possible during a thunderstorm. Because there is always a thunderstorm occurring somewhere on earth, this is one to keep on hand when a storm occurs in your area.

What You Need:
A thunderstorm

What You Do:
1. Explain the concepts behind lightning simply to your students. Lightning occurs when water droplets and ice crystals in clouds are pushed together and torn apart so forcefully that they become charged with electricity.
2. During a thunderstorm, have children count the number of seconds it takes for thunder to sound after seeing a flash of lightning.
3. Help the children figure out how far the lightning is away. (The rule of thumb is that the storm is one mile away for every five seconds' difference.)

Option:
• If you don't want to wait for a storm, have an imaginary one in your classroom. Flash the lights and then count with the children to a designated number. When you reach the number have all of the children clap to make "thunder."

Note:
Share this fact with your children: Approximately 100 lightning bolts strike Earth every second!

RAIN

Let's Sing: Rain Songs

A Moonbow is Just Like a Rainbow
(to the tune of "My Bonnie Lies over the Ocean")

A moonbow is just like a rainbow,
Except that you'll see it at night.
Its colors are in rainbow order,
But they aren't nearly as bright, as bright.

Moonbow, oh, moonbow,
Please color the night sky for me, for me.
Moonbow, oh, moonbow,
Please color the night sky for me!

Do You Like the Rain?
(to the tune of "Do Your Ears Hang Low?")

Do you like the rain
When it hits the window pane?
Do you know rain makes things grow.
And sometimes you'll see rainbows.
Do you like to go outside
When a rainbow fills the sky?
Do you like the rain?

RAIN

Let's Learn: Mother Goose Rhymes

Rain, Rain, Go Away!
Rain, rain, go away!
Come again another day.

When the Dew Is on the Grass
When the dew is on the grass,
Rain will never come to pass.

Comes the Rain Before the Wind
Comes the rain before the wind,
Then your topsail you must mind.
Comes the wind before the rain,
Haul your topsail up again.

Pale Moon Doth Rain
Pale moon doth rain,
Red moon doth blow,
White moon doth neither rain nor snow.

When the Stars Begin to Huddle
When the stars begin to huddle
The earth will soon become a puddle.

Doctor Foster Went to Gloucester
Doctor Foster went to Gloucester
In a shower of rain;
He stepped in a puddle,
Right up to his middle,
And never went there again.

RAIN

Let's Learn: Mother Goose Rhymes

Flour of England, Fruit of Spain

Flour of England, fruit of Spain
Met together in a shower of rain,
Put in a bag and tied round with a string,
If you'll tell me this riddle, I'll give you a ring.
(Answer: a plum pudding)

Rain Before Seven

Rain before seven
Fine before eleven.

Rainbow in the Morning

Rainbow in the morning,
Shipper's warning;
Rainbow at night,
Shipper's delight.
Winter's thunder
Is the world's wonder.

Rainbow in the East

Rainbow in the east,
Sign of a farmer's feast.
Rainbow in the west,
Sign of a farmer's rest.

St. Swithin's Day

St. Swithin's Day if thou dost rain,
For forty days it will remain;
St. Swithin's Day if thou be fair,
For forty days 'twill rain na mair.

"I'M A RAINBOW"

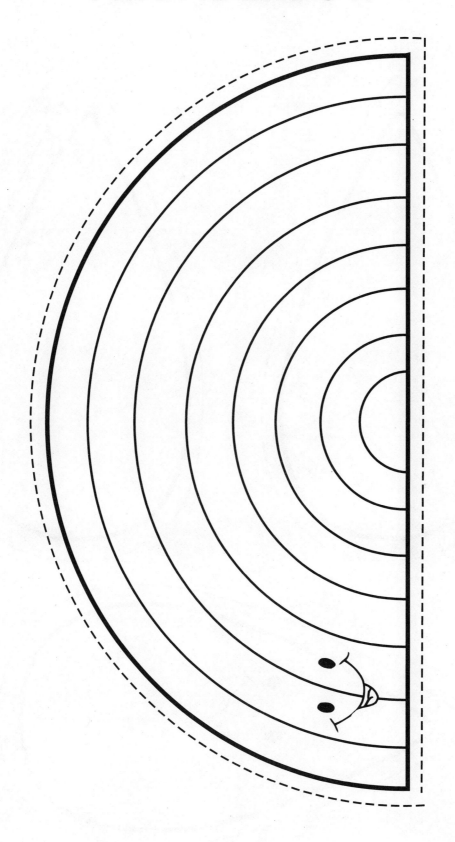

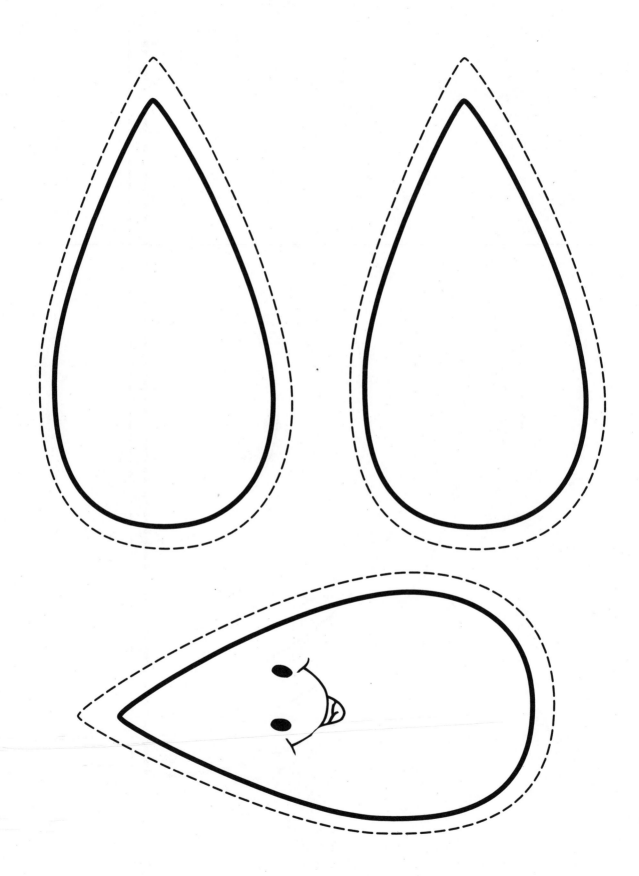

WIND

Introduction

• Let's Read:
The Turnaround Wind by Arnold Lobel (Harper & Row, 1988).
An entire town of people go outside to enjoy fine weather.
When the wind begins to blow, it makes everything topsy-turvy.
Each picture can be viewed upside-down and right-side up!

• Let's Talk:
Take children outside to feel the wind. (Make sure they dress
warmly!) If possible, fly a kite with children on a windy day. If
you are experiencing windless weather, bring a fan into the
classroom and use it to blow paper leaves or pinwheels. Invite
the children to talk about different experiences they have had
with wind. For example, they might have seen leaves blowing
down a street or heard the wind rustling in trees. Ask if the children like the wind or if any have been scared by the "whoooo"
sound of howling wind.

• Let's Learn:
Wind is air in motion. Sometimes the wind moves slowly and
sometimes it moves quickly. A slow wind is called a breeze.
Strong winds can make hurricanes. There are twelve levels of
winds, from one (light air) to twelve (hurricane). Winds blow
when there is a difference in air temperatures. This happens
because the sun heats some parts of the land and water more
than others. Warm air rises and cool air falls (because it is
heavier).

Duplicate four copies of the "I'm the Wind" pattern
(p. 46) and label the patterns "North," "South," "East," and
"West." Use a compass to find the correct direction and post
the patterns in each corner of your room.

WIND

Let's Create: Blow, Wind, Blow Art

Have children blow on their fingers to feel the air. Then have children wet their fingers and blow again. Their fingers will feel cool. Explain that they are acting like the wind!

What You Need:

Watercolors (in containers to share), straws (one per child; label each child's straw with masking tape and a marker), paper, eyedroppers (to share)

What You Do:

1. Explain that the children will be the wind for this activity.
2. Give each child a piece of paper.
3. Have children place droplets of color onto their papers and then blow the colors along their papers using straws.
4. Let children experiment with different colors, mixing them as they wish. (Remind children that too many colors on a single paper may make the pictures look "muddy.")
5. Post the completed pictures on a "Windy Art!" bulletin board.

Book Link:

• *Wind Is to Feel* by Shirley Cook Hatch, illustrated by Marilyn Miller (Coward, 1973).
This book describes many ways that wind affects our lives. Wind blows the smell of freshly cut grass toward us. Wind moves sailboats. Wind cools us down on hot days.

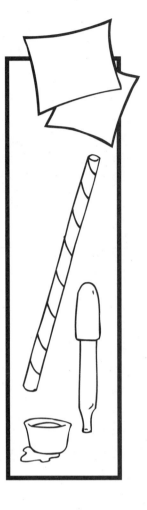

WIND

Let's Create: Wonderful Wind Chimes

Children can make these individually or work together in small groups to create cooperative chimes.

What You Need:

Hangers (one per child), yarn, scissors, construction paper, glue, tape, a variety of craft materials with holes for easy attachment (old keys, metal buttons, paper clips, and so on)

What You Do:

1. If possible, bring in a set of wind chimes to share with children. Explain that wind chimes are hung outside and that when the wind blows the chimes make noise.
2. Give each child a hanger and a few lengths of yarn.
3. Help children tie one end of each piece of yarn to the hanger.
4. Provide craft materials (listed above) for children to fasten to the free ends of the pieces of yarn.
5. When children have finished attaching objects to their hangers, they can cover the bodies of the hangers with colored construction paper.
6. Hang the completed wind chimes where they will be heard.

Note:

Send a note to parents about this activity, requesting odd materials to attach to your chimes, for example, keys, metal hoop earrings, buttons, old cookie cutters, etc. Have parents donate hangers, as well.

Option:

Have children make clay or dough objects to hang from the chimes. Be sure that each item has a hole for easy threading. Bake them and attach them to the hangers.

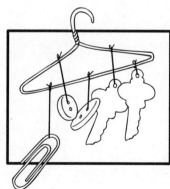

WIND

Let's Find Out: About Wind Instruments

Teach children how to whistle before doing this activity.

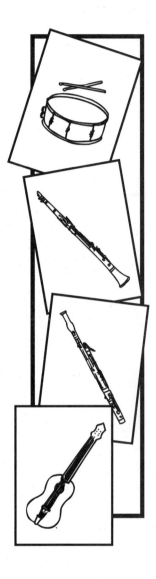

What You Need:
Instrument cards (p. 37), crayons or markers, scissors

What You Do:
1. Duplicate the Instrument cards, color (if desired), and cut out.
2. Discuss different types of musical instruments with the children, for example, guitars, drums, and clarinets. Have children share the names of different instruments they know.
3. Show the children the instrument cards and tell the name of each instrument.
4. Explain that there is a group of instruments called "winds" that make noises when musicians blow "wind" (breath) into them.
5. Have children try to separate the cards that are wind instruments from the cards that aren't.

Options:
• Play different examples of wind instrument recordings, for example, *Peter and the Wolf* by Serge Prokofiev. In this composition, each animal is represented by a different wind instrument.
• Bring in wind instruments for children to observe first-hand.

Book Link:
• *Charlie Parker played be bop* by Chris Raschka (Orchard, 1992).
This book explains the sound of Charlie Parker's music through words and pictures.

INSTRUMENT CARDS

WIND

Let's Find Out: About Sailboats

Wind makes sailboats go. The sail catches the wind and the wind pushes the boat through the water.

What You Need:

Water table or tub of water, floating boats, pipe cleaners, stiff paper, tape, clay

What You Do:

1. Set up a water table.
2. Provide floating boats with sails. (If you don't have any boats with sails, you can make small paper sails using tape and pipe cleaners and attach them to the boats using bits of clay.)
3. Have children set the boats in the water.
4. Have children blow the boats across the water.
5. Ask children questions after they do these two activities. For example, "Did the boats move faster when you blew them or when you didn't?"

Option:

• Have children try blowing corks, empty film canisters, and other floatable objects across the water.

Book Link:

• *Little Fox Goes to the End of the World* by Ann Tompert, illustrated by John Wallner (Crown, 1976).
Little Fox takes an imaginary journey around the world, using a boat and capturing wind in pillowcases.

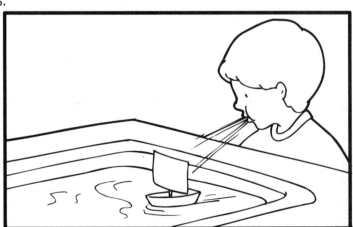

WIND

Let's Find Out: About Wind Directions

We can't see wind, but we can see what wind can do.

What You Need:
Liquid detergent, pipe cleaners (one per child), cups (one per child), water

What You Do:
1. Mix a small amount of liquid detergent and water in each cup.
2. Explain that children cannot see the wind, but they can tell which direction it's blowing by the way things are moved, for example, leaves, dandelion seeds, clouds, windsocks, sailboats, and bubbles.
3. Demonstrate how to bend a pipe cleaner into a bubble wand. One end should be bent into a circle. The rest of the pipe cleaner serves as the handle. Help children who need it.
4. Provide a cup of bubble mixture for each child.
5. Have children dip the end of their pipe cleaners in the mixture and then blow gently to make bubbles.
6. Have children watch which way the bubbles float. Ask children questions as they watch the bubbles, for example, "Which way are the bubbles floating?" (They can simply answer, "That way.") Then ask, "Which way is the wind blowing?" (The answer will be the same.)

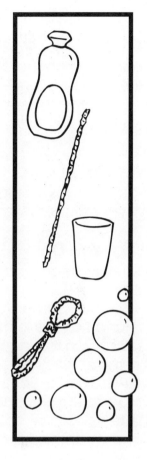

WIND

Let's Play: Blow, Wind, Blow!
Read children the book, *The Runaway Bunny,* by Margaret Wise Brown (Harper and Row, 1942). In it, the mother bunny says she will become the wind and blow her little bunny back home if he tries to sail away from her.

What You Need:
Game Pieces & Spinner (p. 42), Game Board pattern (p. 41), crayons or markers, Contac paper, scissors, hole punch, brad

What You Do:
1. Duplicate the Game Board pattern and the Game Pieces and Spinner.
2. Color all game parts and cover with Contac paper.
3. Punch a hole in the center of the spinner. Cut out the arrow and attach it using a brad.
4. Explain the game to the students. Three players may play at a time. The object of the game is for the children to move their sailboats through the ocean to the final island. The first child spins the spinner and moves to the next similarly shaped spot on the board. The first child to land at the spot marked "end" is the winner.

GAME BOARD PATTERN

41

GAME PIECES & SPINNER

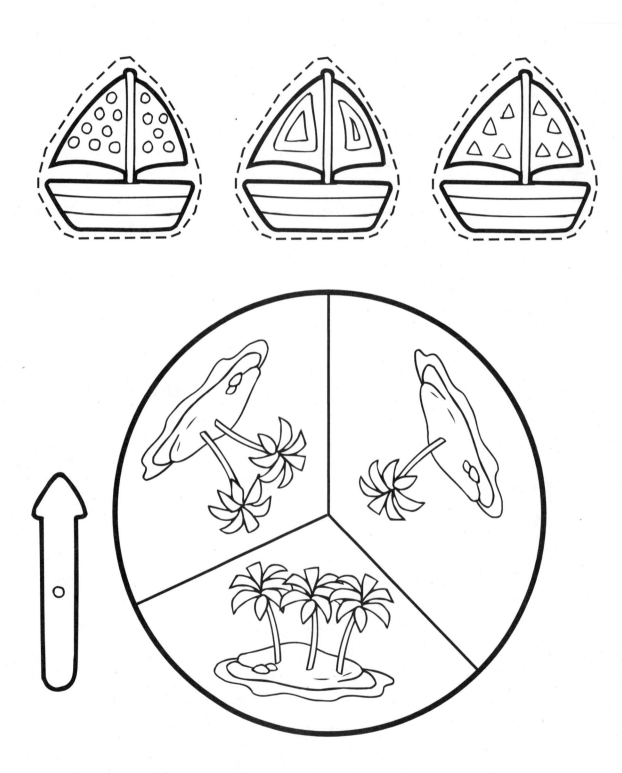

WIND

Let's Sing: Wind Songs

Wind, Wind, Wind, Please Blow
(to the tune of "Row, Row, Row Your Boat")

Wind, wind, wind, please blow,
Fill our sails with air.
With your help, with your help, with your help,
With your help,
We'll sail anywhere!

I'm the North Wind
(to the tune of "Alouette")

I'm the north wind,
Yes, I am the north wind.
I'm the north wind,
I will fill your sails.
When you're on the sea afloat,
I'm the wind that moves your boat.
Sea afloat,
Sea afloat.
Moves your boat,
Moves your boat,
Blooooow!
I'm the north wind,
Yes, I am the north wind.
I'm the north wind,
I will fill your sails.

I'm a Summer Breeze
(to the tune of "Do Your Ears Hang Low?")

I'm a summer breeze,
Not much harder than a sneeze.
I will cool you while you play.
I stir up the leaves all day.
I can rustle through the trees
Just as gentle as you please.
I'm a summer breeze.

WIND

Let's Learn: Mother Goose Rhymes

I Went to the Town

I went to the town,
And whooo went with me?
I went up and down
But nobody could see.
(Answer: the wind)

No Weather Is Ill

No weather is ill,
If the wind be still.

When the Wind Is in the East

When the wind is in the East,
'Tis neither good for man nor beast;
When the wind is in the North,
The skillful fisher goes not forth;
When the wind is in the South,
It blows the bait in the fishes' mouth;
When the wind is in the West,
Then 'tis at the very best.

Blow, Wind, Blow!

Blow, wind, blow! And go, mill, go!
That the miller may grind his corn.
That the baker may take it,
And into rolls make it,
And bring us some hot in the morn.

The South Wind Brings Wet Weather

The south wind brings wet weather,
The north wind wet and cold together;
The west wind always brings us rain,
The east wind blows it back again.

WIND

Let's Learn: Mother Goose Rhymes

My Lady Wind

My Lady Wind, my Lady Wind,
Went round about the house, to find
A chink to get her foot in;
She tried the keyhole in the door,
She tried the crevice in the floor,
And drove the chimney soot in.

And then one night when it was dark,
She blew up such a tiny spark,
That all the house was pothered;
From it she raised such a flame,
As flamed away to Belting Lane,
And White Cross folks were smothered.

And thus when once, my little dears,
A whisper reaches itching ears,
The same will come, you'll find,
Take my advice, restrain your tongue,
Remember what old nurse has sung
Of busy Lady Wind.

The North Wind Doth Blow

The north wind doth blow,
And we shall have snow,
And what will poor robin do then?
Poor thing.

He'll sit in a barn,
And keep himself warm
And hide his head under his wing.
Poor thing.

"I'M THE WIND"

SNOW

Introduction

• Let's Read:

The Story of a Boy Named Will, Who Went Sledding Down the Hill by Daniil Kharms, translated by Jamey Gambrell, illustrated by Vladimir Radunsky (North-South Books).
Will takes a sled ride down a hill, picking up a variety of animals (and a hunter) along the way.

• Let's Talk:

If you live in a part of the country where it snows, have children share their favorite "snowy day" experiences. If you live in states with milder winters, children might share trips they've taken (or trips they'd like to take) to see snow. If possible, show a winter-themed video, or share additional snow-themed books with children.

• Let's Learn:

Snowflakes begin inside the clouds. When it snows, the air must be cold enough to let the flakes fall all the way to the ground without melting. (Rain often begins as snow, but melts as it falls.) Heaviest snowfalls occur when the air is at freezing temperature. A slight rise in temperature can turn the snow to rain.

SNOW

Let's Create: Snowflake Mobiles

All natural snowflakes are six-sided and consist of ice crystals. Snowflakes can be made of one or many crystals of ice.

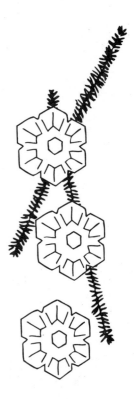

What You Need:
Snowflake patterns (p. 60), white pipe cleaners (cut in half), glue, thread or fishing line, hangers, colored construction paper

What You Do:
1. Duplicate and enlarge the Snowflake patterns to share with the students.
2. Point out the different shapes that snowflakes can be.
3. Provide pipe cleaners for children to use to make snowflakes. They can glue the pieces together to make three-dimensional creations. Children can also simply twist the pipe cleaners to make snowflakes, as well.
4. When the snowflakes have dried, tie them around the middle with pieces of thread or clear fishing line and fasten them to hangers. (Use a few hangers for the class and make cooperative mobiles.)
5. Have children work together to cover the body of the hangers with colored construction paper.
6. Suspend the finished mobiles in your classroom or in a hallway for wintry decoration.

Book Link:
• *Snowflakes* by Joan Sugarman, illustrated by Jennifer Dewey (Little, Brown, 1985).
This is a nonfiction resource explaining what snowflakes are.

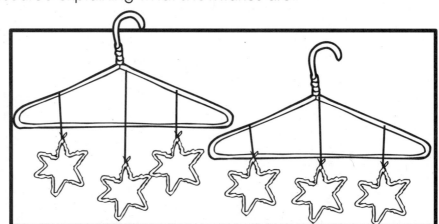

SNOWFLAKE PATTERNS

SNOW

Let's Create: Snowflake Light Catchers

As snowflakes fall, they reflect the light, which makes them look white.

What You Need:

"I'm a Snowflake" pattern (p. 60), heavy paper, tracing paper, scissors, silver glitter, Contac paper, glitter (optional)

What You Do:

1. Duplicate a copy of the "I'm a Snowflake" pattern onto heavy paper for each child. (Or make a few of these stencils for children to share.)
2. Cut the snowflakes out. (Older children may be able to do this themselves.)
3. Have children use the snowflake stencils to trace. They can cut out their traced snowflakes.
4. Seal each snowflake between two sheets of Contac paper. (You might shake a little glitter onto the snowflake before sealing for extra sparkle.)
5. Post the snowflakes in a window.

Book Link:

• *The Snowy Day* by Ezra Jack Keats (Viking, 1962). Peter puts on his snowsuit and spends a day exploring the snow-covered landscape.

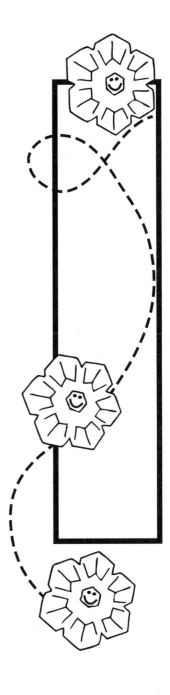

SNOW

Let's Create: Mr. and Mrs. Snow

What You Need:
Colored construction paper, cotton balls, glue, fabric scraps (felt, yarn, lace), white tempera paint, cotton swabs

What You Do:
1. Provide colored construction paper for children to use as the backgrounds for their pictures.
2. Have children glue cotton balls to their papers to make snow people.
3. Children can decorate their pictures using bits of yarn, felt, and lace scraps.
4. Provide tempera paint and cotton swabs for children to use to make snowflakes around their snow people. Children can dip the swabs into the white paint and then dot the swabs on their papers.
5. Post the completed pictures on a "Snow People" bulletin board.

Option:
Provide wiggly eyes for children to glue to their snow people.

Book Link:
• *The Snowman* by Raymond Briggs (Random House, 1978). This wordless book is about a boy and the snowman he builds. When the snowman comes to life, the boy takes him on a tour of his house.

SNOW

Let's Create: A Special Snowflake Mural

What You Need:
"I'm a Snowflake" pattern (p. 60), photographs of the children, scissors, glue, butcher paper, large marker

What You Do:
1. Ask parents to send photos of their children to school. These photos will be used in an art project, so they should not be originals. (Or you can duplicate the photos on a photocopier and return originals to parents.)
2. Duplicate a copy of the "I'm a Snowflake" pattern for each child.
3. Have each child cut his or her face out of the photograph and glue it to the center of the "I'm a Snowflake" pattern.
4. Once the snowflakes have dried, have children glue them to a large sheet of butcher paper.
5. Print the words "No Two Are Alike" on the mural. Write each child's name under his or her snowflake picture.
6. Post the mural in your room or in a hallway as decoration.

Book Link:
• *White Snow Bright Snow* by Alvin Tresselt, illustrated by Roger Duvoisin (Lothrop, 1947).
This Caldecott Award winner focuses on the time period from winter to spring. In it, children catch snowflakes on their tongues, have a snowball fight, and build a snow fort.

SNOW

Let's Find Out: About Snow-white Foxes

Foxes are relatives of dogs. Some foxes live in the arctic. They have gray fur during three seasons. During winter, their coats change to white. This change helps them blend in with the snow.

What You Need:
Fox pattern (p. 54), gray crayons, white construction paper, scissors, tape

What You Do:
1. Duplicate one copy of the Fox pattern for each child.
2. Help children cut out the foxes.
3. Have the children trace the patterns onto sheets of white construction paper and color the traced foxes gray.
4. Demonstrate how to tape the white pattern on top of the gray fox using one "hinge" of tape.
5. Ask the children which fox blends in better with the white background, the gray fox or the white fox.

Option:
Discuss other animals who use camouflage colors to blend in.

Book Link:
• *Animal Camouflage: A Closer Look* by Joyce Powzyk (Bradbury, 1990).
This book shows animal and insect camouflage techniques.

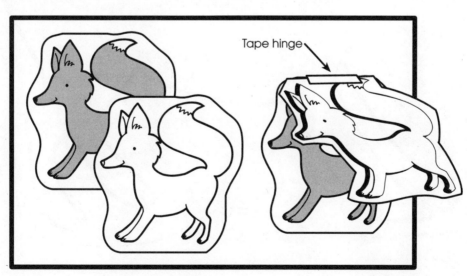

Tape hinge

SNOW

Let's Play: Snowflake Race

What You Need:
Game Board pattern (p. 56), Game Cards (p. 57), Game Markers (bottom of this page), scissors, clear Contac paper, crayons or markers

What You Do:
1. Duplicate the Game Board pattern, the Game Markers, and the Game Cards.
2. Color each different snowflake background a different color to help children tell them apart. (Do this for both the game cards and the game board. When children pick a red card, they will know to move to the next red snowflake on the board.) Color the Game Markers, as well.
3. Cover all game pieces with Contac paper.
4. Teach children how to play the game. They will pick a card and then move to the next similarly shaped colored snowflake on the game board. They will know which square to move to based on the shape of the snowflake and the color. The first child to reach the spot marked "end" is the winner. (If a child is near the end, and picks a card that he or she doesn't need, the next child takes a turn.)

GAMEBOARD

GAME CARDS

SNOW

Let's Sing: Snow Songs

I'm a Little Snowflake
(to the tune of "I'm a Little Teapot")

I'm a little snowflake.
You can see,
No other snowflake
Looks like me.
You can pick me up
After I fall.
Roll me with my friends
To make snowballs!

I'm a Snowflake
(to the tune of "Alouette")

I'm a snowflake.
Yes, I am a snowflake.
I'm a snowflake,
I fall from the sky.
No two snowflakes look the same.
That's part of a snowflake's fame.
Look the same,
Look the same.
Snowflake's fame,
Snowflake's fame.
Snooooow.
I'm a snowflake.
Yes, I am a snowflake.
I'm a snowflake.
I fall from the sky.

SNOW

Let's Learn: Mother Goose Rhymes

White Bird Featherless

*White bird featherless
Flew from Paradise,
Pitched on the castle wall;
Along came Lord Landless,
Took it up handless
To the King's White Hall.*
(Answer: snow)

Cold and Raw

*Cold and raw the north wind doth blow
Bleak in the morning early,
All the hills are covered with snow,
And winter's now come fairly.*

Cuckoo, Cherry Tree

*Cuckoo, cherry tree.
Catch a bird, and give it to me;
Let the tree be high or low,
Let it hail, rain, or snow.*

59

"I'M A SNOWFLAKE"

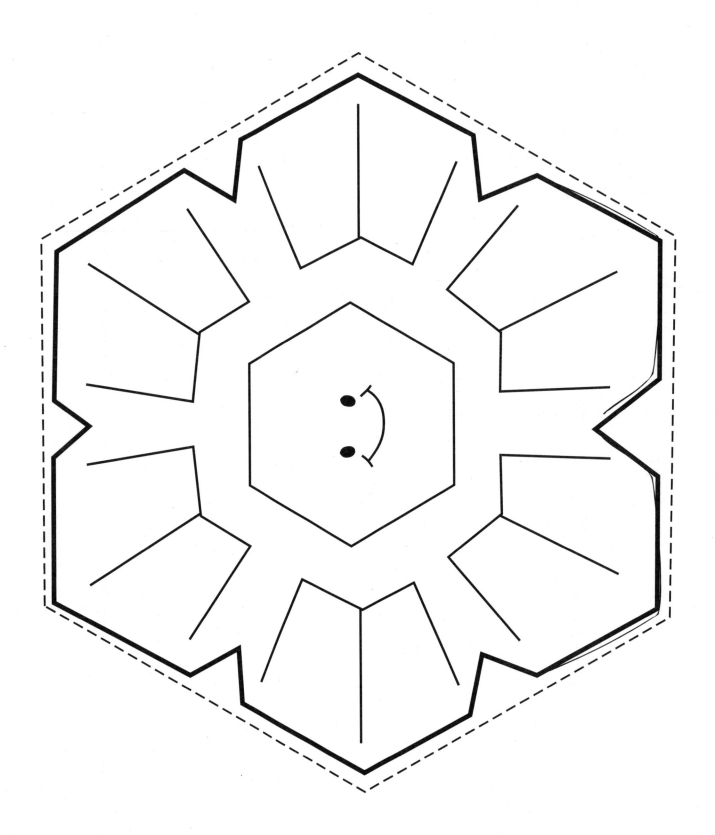

SUNNY DAYS

Introduction

• Let's Read:
How the Sun Was Brought Back to the Sky by Mirra Ginsburg, illustrated by Jose Aruego and Ariane Dewey (Macmillan, 1975). After three cloudy days, the sun forgets how to shine. Luckily, a group of chicks and their other animal friends visit sun's house and make it shine again!

• Let's Talk:
Have children share their feelings about sunny days versus rainy days. Would they be happy if the sun shined all the time? Have children share the different activities they like to do on sunny days. Make a class list of things to do on sunny days, for example, go to the beach, go swimming, play in the park, have a picnic, visit the zoo, and so on. Choose an activity to do as a class on a warm, sunny day. Remind children to wear sunglasses and a hat when it's very sunny and to always put on sunscreen when they go outside!

• Let's Learn:
Sunny weather and cloudless skies are common over much of the world, especially during the summer. Sunny weather is the most stable kind of weather. A day that begins sunny and cloudless will most likely stay that way. The sky doesn't become dark immediately after the sun sets. This is because sunlight continues to illuminate the air overhead. A twilight glow can remain in the west even an hour after sunset!

Remind children to **NEVER** look directly at the sun. Doing so can cause permanent eye damage!

SUNNY DAYS

Let's Create: A Window of Sunshine

At the back of the book, *How the Sun Was Brought Back to the Sky*, there is a drawing of a window. If possible, show children this picture before introducing this activity.

What You Need:
Butcher paper, tempera paint, paintbrushes, easels, smocks (one per child)

What You Do:
1. Cut one window shape (rectangle) from butcher paper for each child.
2. Set the papers on easels along with the tempera paint and paintbrushes.
3. Have the children imagine they are looking out of a window on a sunny day.
4. Have the children paint what they "see" out of their imaginary windows.
5. Post the completed pictures in a row at the children's eye level. Let them walk by the windows and observe what their friends have painted.

SUNNY DAYS

Let's Create: Beach Scenes

Read a book about the beach before embarking on this activity.
The Seashore Book by Charlotte Zolotow, illustrated by Wendell Minor (HarperCollins, 1992) is a beautiful beach book.

What You Need:

Sand (in small containers), construction paper, glue, seashell-shaped pasta, crayons or markers, newsprint

What You Do:

1. Cover the work area with newsprint.
2. Have children draw beach scenes on sheets of construction paper.
3. Provide seashell-shaped pasta and sand for children to glue to their beach pictures.Children can spread glue on their papers and then sprinkle the sand on the glue. They can glue the pasta on top of the sand.
4. Have the children shake excess sand onto the newsprint.

Options:

• Provide a variety of different shades of colored sand for children to glue to their pictures instead of regular sand.
• Mix gold glitter with sand to make it sparkle.

Two Ways to Make Colored Sand:

• Swirl a piece of colored chalk in a small cup of sand. The chalk will rub off and color the sand.
• Mix powdered tempera paint with small containers of sand to color it.

Let's Create: Glorious Auroras

Auroras are luminous, colored lights in the night sky that occur occasionally. They appear when blasts from the sun's surface enter Earth's atmosphere. The aurora borealis are visible from the Arctic Circle. The aurora australis are visible at the Antarctic Circle.

What You Need:
Black construction paper, colored chalk, felt scraps or sponges

What You Do:
1. Explain to the children what auroras are. If possible, show a picture (see Book Links, below).
2. Provide black construction paper and colored chalk for children to use to create their own auroras.
3. Have the children blend the colors together using pieces of felt or dry sponges.
4. Spray the completed pictures with hair spray, a great chalk fixative. (Do this away from the children.)
5. Post the pictures on an "Amazing Auroras" bulletin board.

Book Links:
• *Aurora: The Mysterious Northern Lights* by Candace Sherk Savage (Sierra Club Books, 1994).
• *The Aurora Watchers Handbook* by Neil T. Davis (University of Alaska Press, 1992).

SUNNY DAYS

Let's Create: Shadow Friends

These friends will stay with children all the time! You might have children do the "Let's Find Out" activity (p. 68) before they create these pictures.

What You Need:

Butcher paper, crayons or markers, sunlight, scissors

What You Do:

1. On a sunny day, take the children outside.
2. Divide the children into pairs and give each child a long sheet of butcher paper. (The papers should be slightly taller than the children.)
3. Have the children take turns tracing their shadows. Have the children place their papers on smooth concrete. One child stands so that his or her shadow falls on the sheet of paper. The other child traces the shadow. The children then switch jobs on new pieces of paper.
4. The children can take their shadows inside, color them using crayons or markers, and cut them out.
5. Post the completed pictures around the classroom. Label each picture with the name of the child who created it, for example, "Tanya's Shadow."

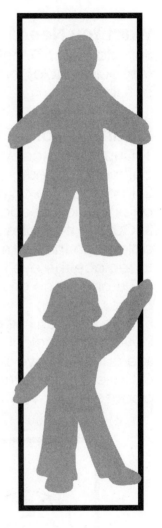

Book Link:

• *In Shadowland* by Mitsumasa Anno (Orchard, 1988). "Suppose there was a land of shadows," begins this book. Supposing their is one, Anno has certainly captured it!

SUNNY DAYS

Let's Create: Sun Masks

In ancient times, people depended on the sun even more than we do today. They needed sun for light and heat and for making sure their crops grew. Many ancient peoples prayed to a sun god!

What You Need:

Sun Mask (p. 67), hole punch, scissors, yarn, crayons or markers (especially gold), hole reinforcers (four for each child) or pieces of tape

What You Do:

1. Duplicate a copy of the Sun Mask pattern for each child to color and cut out.
2. Punch a hole on each side of the mask and place a reinforcer on each side of each hole.
3. Cut out the holes for the children's eyes. (Older children will be able to do this themselves.) Or cut a rectangular slit on each mask to replace the eye holes.
4. Tie one piece of yarn to each hole. (Each mask will have two pieces of yarn.)
5. Help children put on their masks. Tie the two pieces of yarn in a bow at the back of each child's head. (Make sure children can see out of the eye slit.)
6. Have children wear their masks while performing the songs about sun (pp. 70-71) for other students, friends, or family.

SUN MASK

SUNNY DAYS

Let's Find Out: About Shadows
In this activity, children will be going on a Shadow Hunt!

What You Need:
Sunlight

What You Do:
1. Explain that everyone has a shadow and tell children that they will be trying to find theirs. (It isn't difficult!)
2. On a sunny afternoon, take the children outside.
3. Once the children have found their shadows, challenge them to try to outsmart their shadows. For example, Can they outrun their shadows? Can they lose their shadows?
4. Have children look for at least five shadows made by other objects, for example, a tree, a bench, another child, a car, a telephone pole, and so on.
5. Bring the children back inside. Have children share the different shadows they saw outside.

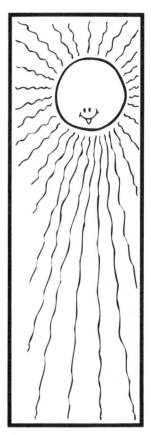

Option:
• Explain that night is a shadow. The sun shines on one side of the earth at a time. When the sun is shining on us, it is night on the other side of the earth. When we have day, the other side of the earth is in shadow.

Book Link:
• *Shadow Magic* by Seymour Simon, illustrated by Stella Ormai (Lothrop, 1985).
This book explains what shadows are and how they are formed. It also tells how to make a sundial and a shadow show.

SUNNY DAYS

Let's Play: Shadow Games

What You Need:
A lamp

What You Do:
1. Set a lamp in the mostly darkened room.
2. Position the children so that they are between the lamp and the wall. Have them hold up their hands to make shadows on the wall.
3. Children can experiment moving closer or farther away from the lamp to make their shadows bigger and smaller.
4. Show children how to position their fingers to make different animal shapes. They can hold up two fingers to make a rabbit with tall ears. If they link their thumbs together and outstretch their fingers, they can make birds or butterflies. Have them see what other shapes they can make!

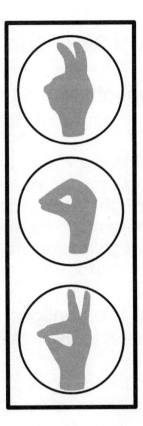

Option:
• Hang a sheet from a clothesline stretched across the room. Project a light from behind it and have a few children make shadows (between the lamp and the sheet) for the rest of the children to enjoy.

Book Link:
• *Shadow Play* by Paul Fleischman, illustrated by Eric Beddows (Harper and Row, 1990).
In this variation of Beauty and the Beast, the story is retold as a shadow play at a country fair.

SUNNY DAYS

Let's Sing: Sun Songs

Sunlight Makes Things Grow
(to the tune of "Bingo")

In the sky, the warm sun shines,
And sunlight makes things grow.
Sunlight makes things grow.
Sunlight makes things grow.
Sunlight makes things grow.
The sunlight makes things grow.

I'm the Sunlight
(to the tune of "Alouette")

I'm the sunlight.
Yes, I am the sunlight.
I'm the sunlight.
I make the world warm.
I shine down upon the Earth.
I help grow things from the dirt.
On the Earth.
On the Earth.
From the dirt.
From the dirt.
Grooooow!
I'm the sunlight.
Yes, I am the sunlight.
I'm the sunlight.

I make the world warm.

SUNNY DAYS

Let's Sing: Sun Songs

Take Me Out in the Sunshine
(to the tune of "Take Me Out to the Ball Game")

Take me out in the sunshine.
Take me out to the beach.
I want to soak up some golden rays.
I want to see the sun shining for days.

Because sunlight helps all the plants grow,
Our vegetables, flowers, and trees.
So let's give a cheer for the sun,
It grows plants we need.

We Need the Sunshine
(to the tune of "You Are My Sunshine")

We need the sunshine,
The golden sunshine.
The sun helps grow plants,
And foods we eat.
The sunlight's power
Is so important.
The sunshine's energy gives us our heat.

SUNNY DAYS

Let's Learn: Mother Goose Rhymes

For All the Evil Under the Sun
For all the evil under the sun,
There is a remedy, or there is none.
If there be one, try and find it;
If there be none, never mind it.

If Candlemas Day Be Fair and Bright
If Candlemas Day be fair and bright,
Winter will have another flight;
If on Candlemas Day it be shower and rain,
Winter is gone, and will not come again.

Rain on Monday
Rain on Monday,
Sunshine next Sunday.

Through Storm and Wind
Through storm and wind,
Sunshine and shower,
Still will ye find
Groundel in flower.

A Sunshiny Shower
A sunshiny shower
Won't last half an hour

"I'M THE SUN"

WEATHER ICONS

Let children help you keep track of the weather each month. Duplicate and enlarge the Calendar patterns (pp. 76-77) each month, write in the numbers for each day of the week, and fill in the name of the month at the top. Duplicate the weather icons and weather gear icons (p. 75).

Have children help you choose patterns each day. For example, if it's raining, children can choose the rain pattern plus the galoshes or umbrella patterns to place on the calendar.

WEATHER GEAR ICONS

CALENDAR PATTERN

SUNDAY	MONDAY	TUESDAY	WEDNESDAY

CALENDAR PATTERN

WEDNESDAY	THURSDAY	FRIDAY	SATURDAY

STORYBOOK RESOURCES

Cloud and Fog Books:
• *Cloudy with a Chance of Meatballs* by Judi Barrett (Atheneum, 1978).
The townspeople of Chewandswallow enjoy having their meals come down from the sky. In this town, it rains soup and juice and snows mashed potatoes. But when odd weather hits the town, it makes for some pretty ridiculous meals!
• *Fog Drift Morning* by Deborah Kogan Ray (Harper & Row, 1983).
A girl and her mother enjoy a fog-filled morning.
• *Small Cloud* by Ariane, illustrated by Annie Gusman (Unicorn, 1984).
This is the tale of the birth of a cloud.

Rain Books:
• *Bringing the Rain to Kapiti* Plain, retold by Verna Aardema, illustrated by Beatriz Vidal (Dial, 1981).
This African tale is retold as a cumulative rhyme.
• *Mushroom in the Rain* by Mirra Ginsburg, illustrated by Jose Aruego and Ariane Dewey (Macmillan, 1974).
A mushroom houses a variety of wet animals during a storm.
• *The Rain Door* by Russell Hoban (Thomas Y. Crowell, 1986).
On a hot summer day, Harry follows a mysterious rag-and-bone man through a magical "Rain Door," discovering where thunder and lightning come from.

Snow Books:
• *The Big Snow* by Berta and Elmer Hader (Macmillan, 1948).
The animals in the woods and meadow know that when the geese fly south, the snow will come soon.
• *First Snow* by Emily Arnold McCully (Harper & Row, 1985).
This wordless book shows a mouse family enjoying a day in the snow.
• *Katy and the Big Snow* by Virginia Lee Burton (Houghton Mifflin, 1943).
Katy, a crawler tractor, gets the job of plowing through the snow to rescue the city of Geoppolis.

STORYBOOK RESOURCES

Seasonal Weather Books:

• *Can't Sit Still* by Karen E. Lotz, illustrated by Colleen Browning (Dutton, 1993).
A young girl experiences all four seasons in the city. She plays in the autumn leaves, makes "animal" tracks in the snow, climbs up to the roof in the springtime rain, and plays hopscotch on the pavement during the summer.
• *Frog and Toad All Year* by Arnold Lobel (Harper, 1976).
Frog and Toad are good friends who spend time together all year long. This "I Can Read Book" has five chapters, with stories appropriate for different kinds of weather: snow, rain, sun, wind, and a bonus holiday tale.
• *The Happy Day* by Ruth Krauss, illustrated by Marc Simont (HarperTrophy, 1949).
Field mice, bears, snails, squirrels, and groundhogs sleep through the winter. The smell of the first spring flower wakes them up.
• *The House of Four Seasons* by Roger Duvoisin (Lothrop, 1956).
A family buys a house in the country. As they fix it up, their children learn about both colors and seasons.

Sunny Day Books:

• *Dawn* by Uri Shulevitz (Farrar, 1974).
As you turn the pages of this book, the children will be able to witness the sky changing colors and night becoming day.
• *Who Gets the Sun Out of Bed?* by Nancy White Carlstrom, illustrated by David McPhail (Little, 1992).
On a cold winter morning, the lazy sun is reluctant to rise. Who will wake him up? The moon tries, and so does a bunny named Midnight and a little boy named Nicholas.

Wind Books:

• *Gilberto and the Wind* by Marie Hall Ets (Viking, 1963).
Gilberto is friends with the wind. Sometimes Wind is helpful, but sometimes it scares Gilberto.
• *The Wind Thief* by Diane Dawson (Atheneum, 1977).
The mighty wind decides he needs a hat and attempts to blow one away from a little boy. The wind ends up with more hats than he expected!

NONFICTION RESOURCES

Rain Books:
• *Rain & Hail* by Franklyn M. Branley
(Thomas Y. Crowell, 1963).
This informative book traces the water cycle, explaining why water evaporates, how clouds form, and how and why water falls back to the ground as rain.

Shadow Books:
• *What Makes a Shadow?* by Clyde Robert Bulla, illustrated by Adrienne Adams (Scholastic, 1962).
Informative book about what shadows are and how to find them.

Weather Books:
• *Exploring the Sky by Day: The Equinox Guide to Weather and the Atmosphere* by Terrence Dickinson
(Camden House, 1988).
This factual resource has many color photographs to share with students.
• *Weather* by Brian Cosgrove (Knopf, 1991).
This Eyewitness book is filled with fascinating information about all sorts of weather, from sunny days to tropical storms!